CONTENTS

£7.99

INDIANA JONES
TIMELINE

1899	• Henry 'Indiana' Jones Jr is born
1912	• Mother dies
1916	• Quits school • Joins the Mexican revolution • Fights in First World War
1918	• Attends University of Chicago, studies archaeology under Professor Abner Ravenwood alongside Harold Oxley
1922	• Graduates and goes to study linguistics in Paris
1925	• First teaching job at London University
1926	• Joins Abner Ravenwood on a dig in Jerusalem • Briefly romances Abner's daughter Marion
1935	• Foils a plot by the Thuggee cult to steal the Sankara stones
1936	• Asked by US Government to find the Ark of the Covenant • Is reunited with Marion Ravenwood
1937	• Leaves Marion Ravenwood shortly before their planned wedding
1938	• Finds the Holy Grail
1939–1945	• Second World War • Spies for the Office of Strategic Services • Meets M16 agent George 'Mac' McHale
1957	• Runs afoul the Soviets searching for the crystal skull of Akator

INDIANA JONES

Dr Henry 'Indiana' Jones Jr is an American archaeologist, professor and adventurer. He has found several famous mythological artefacts and met many important historical figures. He has worked with armed forces and intelligence agencies all around the world, but his first love has always been archaeology.

When he was a little boy, Indiana's parents took him on a world tour, and this was when his interest in history really began. When the family returned home, Indy's mother became ill and died. His father buried himself in his studies, and they grew further and further apart.

Indy left school when he was seventeen and travelled around the world, becoming involved in a revolution in Mexico and then fighting in the First World War. When the war ended he went to university and studied archaeology, but nothing could squash his adventurous spirit. As he grew older, he began to combine his teaching job with exciting missions to far-flung corners of the planet.

Now a respected professor of archaeology, Indy continues to seek out rare artefacts and sacred treasures, some of which are thought to be myths. His searches often bring him into conflict with people and groups who want to find a quick route to ultimate power. Indy has faced death many times, but his courage, humour and intelligence have always saved the day!

MARION
RAVENWOOD

Marion Ravenwood was born in 1909, the daughter of the famous archaeologist and treasure-hunter, Abner Ravenwood. In 1925 she began a relationship with Indiana Jones, but her father did not approve and Indy left. Years later she was engaged to Indy, but he left her a week before the wedding and she would not see him again for many long years. Marion is fiercely independent, very intelligent and extremely stubborn. She and Indy had a fiery relationship, but she has never forgotten him.

HAROLD
OXLEY (OX)

Harold Oxley was born in England in 1887. While studying archaeology under Abner Ravenwood at the University of Chicago, he made friends with Indiana Jones. In 1937 Oxley broke off their friendship after Indiana left Marion Ravenwood.

Oxley is obsessively interested in the crystal skulls of ancient legend, and he has recently focused his investigations on South America.

MUTT
WILLIAMS

Mutt is Marion Ravenwood's son. He models himself on his favourite film stars – Marlon Brando and James Dean – and spends all his time working on motorcycles. His bike is his pride and joy. Mutt has dropped out of school, but he is a skilled fencer and he loves reading. He shares Indy's love of adventure, and has the same reckless, daredevil spirit.

OBTAINER OF RARE ANTIQUITIES

Indiana Jones

TRUSTED SINCE

GEORGE
McHALE (MAC)

Mac is an archaeologist and an old friend of Indy's. They met during the Second World War, when they were both working for military intelligence. Mac saved Indy's life when they met and Indy has never forgotten how much he owes to Mac. Mac loves gambling and the good life, and he cares more about money than Indy ever could. His greed sometimes leads him to make rash decisions.

DR IRINA
SPALKO

Dr Irina Spalko grew up in a small mountain village in the Ukrainian Soviet Socialist Republic. She has psychic powers and never fit in with the other villagers. As soon as she was old enough, she left the village forever.

Spalko joined the Soviet secret police and took part in experiments in psychic abilities, becoming a highly respected officer. She is a cold-hearted woman who is trained in many forms of combat. She has no pity and only cares what others can do for her. Above all, she is obsessed with improving her psychic powers and knowledge.

ANTONIN
DOVCHENKO

Antonin Dovchenko is a Russian colonel and Dr Spalko's right-hand man. He is cruel and enjoys inflicting pain on others. His immense strength and physical fitness help him to defeat all opponents. He controls his soldiers through fear and violence, but is passionately loyal to his country.

RAIDERS OF THE LOST ARK

I n 1936, Dr Indiana Jones found himself in Peru, seeking an ancient idol. However, after risking his life to recover the treasure, it was stolen by his long-time enemy, a fellow archaeologist called Belloq. Belloq had no scruples, but he had plenty of weapons, and Indy had to return home empty-handed.

Back in the US, Army Intelligence visited Indy.

"The Nazis have teams of archaeologists running around the world looking for all kinds of religious artefacts," they told him. "Right now, there's some kind of German archaeological dig going on in the desert outside Cairo."

Indy worked out that the Nazis had discovered Tanis, the resting place of the Ark of the Covenant. The Ark contained the Ten Commandments, and its power could wipe out entire armies.

"Army Intelligence wants you to get a hold of the Ark before the Nazis do," Marcus Brody told Indy.

Indy went to Nepal and visited a bar that was run by his ex-girlfriend, Marion Ravenwood. Her father, Dr Abner Ravenwood, had owned the headpiece of the Staff of Ra that would guide Indy to the Ark's exact resting place. Marion lied and said that she didn't have the medallion, and Indy left. But then the Nazis arrived!

"What do you want?" Marion asked them.

"The same thing Dr Jones wanted," said Toht, a Nazi torturer.

He threatened Marion with a boiling-hot poker! Just then, Indy returned and saved Marion, setting the bar on fire in the process.

Toht spotted the headpiece on the floor and grabbed it, but it had become red hot in the fire. The boiling-hot medallion burned an imprint of itself on to his palm! Then Indy grabbed the medallion, and Marion, and escaped.

Indy and Marion travelled to Cairo and met up with Indy's friend Sallah. But the Nazis found out that Indy had arrived! After a high-speed chase through the streets of Cairo, Marion was captured and stuffed into a basket on the back of a truck carrying explosives to the site of the Nazi dig. Indy fired his revolver at the driver and the truck crashed and exploded!

Indy was grief-stricken. Marion was dead – how could he possibly go on? But his old enemy Belloq was leading the dig for the Nazis and they were close to finding the Ark. Indy had to stop them.

The Nazis, under the command of an officer called Dietrich, were using the image that was burned on to Toht's hand, but they were digging a mile away from the true site. Indy crept into the Nazi camp and used the medallion to find the exact position of the resting place of the Ark. Better than that, he found Marion – she was alive!

Marion's delight at seeing Indy changed to fury when he refused to free her.

"Jones, you get me out of here!" she yelled. "Come on, Jones! Are you crazy?"

But Indy could not risk letting the Nazis know that he was there!

Indy led his friend Sallah and a team of diggers to the real location of the Ark. They dug all night until they hit stone. They had found the entrance! Suddenly Sallah gave a yell. The floor was covered with snakes!

"Snakes," Indy groaned. "Why did it have to be snakes?"

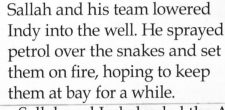

Sallah and his team lowered Indy into the well. He sprayed petrol over the snakes and set them on fire, hoping to keep them at bay for a while.

Sallah and Indy loaded the Ark into a crate and it was pulled up to the surface. Indy waited, but the rope was not sent back down for him. Then he heard a familiar laugh. It was Belloq!

"So once again, Jones, what was briefly yours is now mine," Belloq chuckled. "What a fitting end to your life's pursuits. You're about to become a permanent addition to this archaeological find. But we do not wish to leave you all alone..."

Then, the Nazis accompanying Belloq threw Marion down into the pit and sealed the entrance!

Indy knew that as soon as the torches went out, the snakes would attack. Then he saw some snakes sliding through several holes in a high wall. If the snakes could get in, surely they could get out?

INDIANA JONES

"How the hell are we going to get out of here?" Marion shrieked as snakes slithered towards her.

"I'm working on it!" Indy growled.

"Whatever you're doing, do it faster!" yelled Marion.

Indy toppled a huge statue over and knocked a hole in the wall. Then he and Marion escaped as the last of the torches went out.

Indy risked his life and managed to get the Ark back, but he still had to get it to America. He arranged to travel on a tramp steamer and heaved a sigh of relief as they set off. He had beaten Belloq and the Nazis once and for all! Indy and Marion got some well-earned rest.

Indy was awoken by the sound of the engines stopping. He knew that was a bad sign. Sure enough, the ship was boarded by German soldiers! The Nazis took the Ark and Marion on to their U-boat, but Indy managed to smuggle himself aboard without being spotted.

The Nazi U-boat travelled to a remote island. Belloq had planned a secret ritual to reveal the contents of the Ark. The Nazis set the Ark on an altar

and Indy knew he had to do something! But before he could move, he was taken prisoner and tied up with Marion.

As Belloq began the ceremony, two soldiers removed the lid of the Ark. Ghostly apparitions began to emerge from it. Then a shaft of blinding light rose up.

"Marion, don't look at it, no matter what happens!" yelled Indy, shutting his eyes.

He knew that if they looked, they would be destroyed!

"It's beautiful!" cried Belloq.

Suddenly jets of flame shot into the crowd of soldiers, killing them all instantly. The Nazi officers melted into a pool of goo and Belloq exploded in flames. A shaft of fire rocketed high into the sky and then dropped back down into the Ark, which sealed itself shut.

A few days later, Indy handed over the Ark to government officials.

"You've done your country a great service," they told him.

As Indy walked off with Marion, he just hoped that they would research the Ark properly. It was a source of unspeakable power, and it had given him one of his most exciting adventures!

PATTERN PICKER

Indy needs your help to complete these pattern sequences he has found on the wall of an underground cave. Look carefully at the patterns. Can you work out which shapes will come next? Draw them in and complete the patterns.

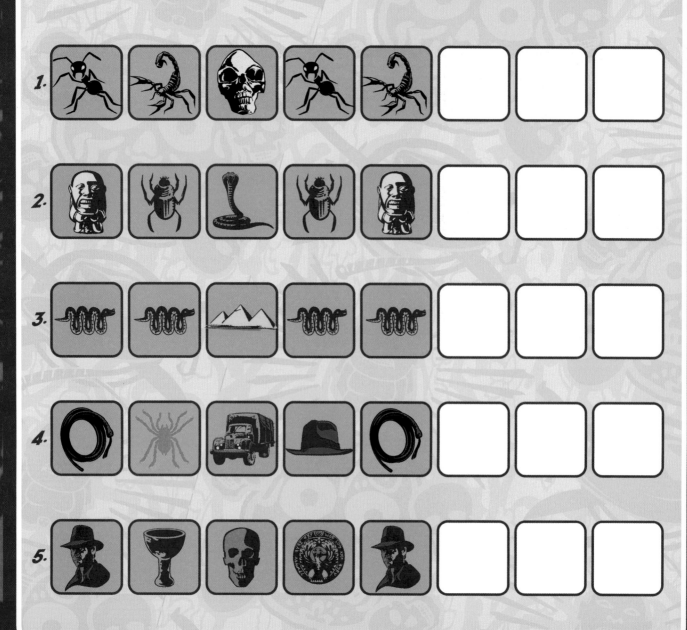

SECRET SCRAMBLE

INDY HAS RECEIVED SOME MESSAGES, BUT ALL THE LETTERS ARE JUMBLED UP. CAN YOU PUT THE LETTERS INTO THE RIGHT ORDER AND READ THE MESSAGES?

Note 1

READ DINY.

HTE CRESET SURETREA SI BEDURI NI ERUP.

ROFM ACM.

Note 2

OT IANANDI JEONS.

EWBEAR! OUY REA NI GRTEA DNGAER!

A FNDRIE.

Note 3

TEH NSAZI AVHE FUNOD YM DINHIG APLCE. SVEA EM. IYND!

Note 4

RD JESON, OYU ILWL RNVEE DSUCECE.

Note 5

IORJUN.

EKPE HITS DAIRY FESA. OD OTN ETL TI UTO FO RYOU GSIHT!

ADD

MAZE MUDDLE

Can you help Indy to reach the crystal skull of Akator before the evil Irina Spalko? Find the quickest way through the maze!

START

CROSSWORD

SOLVE THE CLUES AND FILL IN THE ANSWERS TO DISCOVER THE NAME OF ONE OF INDY'S ENEMIES.

1. What is Marion's father's first name?

2. In which country does Indy find the Ark of the Covenant?

3. Which of Indy's friends has always obsessed with finding the crystal skull?

4. What subject does Indy teach?

5. In India, Indy helps to rescue the Sankara _____.

6. What word describes the search for the Holy Grail?

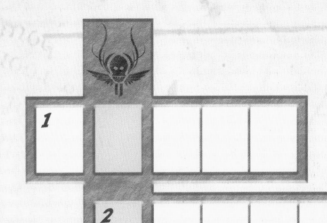

THE TEMPLE OF DOOM

A year before his Ark adventure, Indy was in a Shanghai nightclub called Obi-Wan. The beautiful singer Willie Scott was performing, but Indy was there to meet some Chinese men and their boss, Lao Che. Lao Che gave Indy a huge diamond in return for an artefact he had found, but he didn't really want to pay. He poisoned Indy and then offered him the antidote – in exchange for the diamond!

Indy started a fight and suddenly there was pandemonium in the nightclub! People raced for the doors as Indy lunged for the antidote. It skidded across the floor and into the sea of people. Then Willie picked it up. Indy grabbed her and pulled her out of the window!

They landed in a car, driven by Indy's sidekick, Short Round. They headed to a nearby airport, where they boarded a plane. Unfortunately, Lao Che owned it! While their passengers slept, the pilots dumped the remaining fuel and parachuted out of the plane.

Just in time, Indy woke up. He grabbed a self-inflating emergency raft and told Willie and Shorty to hold on. It was their only chance! Indy, Willie and Shorty leaped from the plane, clinging to the raft. They landed on the snowy Indian mountain below, and hurtled down the mountainside.

After surviving the harrowing trip down the mountain, they landed in a fast-moving river. By now Willie had completely lost her temper.

"I hate the water!" she yelled at Indy. "And I hate being wet! And I hate you!"

"Good!" Indy bellowed.

Soon they reached a village. The villagers believed that they were cursed, and said that evil spirits had taken their children away because their sacred Sankara stone was stolen. They begged Indy to find their lost children, and said that Pankot Palace was at the heart of the mystery.

"Pankot?" shrieked Willie. "I can't go to Pankot! I'm a singer!"

Indy ignored her and agreed to help.

"I was happy in Shanghai," Willie wailed as she climbed on to a smelly elephant. "I had a little house and a garden. My friends were rich. We went to parties all the time!"

Indy, Short Round and Willie set off towards Pankot Palace.

When they arrived at the palace, Indy, Shorty and Willie were invited to dinner with the Maharajah. Everyone was very polite to them, but that night a soldier attacked Indy in his room. Indy soon dealt with him, but it was clear that they were in danger. Indy and Shorty dashed into Willie's room to check that she was safe.

When Indy searched Willie's room for assassins, he discovered a hidden passage! Indy and Shorty stepped into the tunnel, and soon found themselves in a large chamber. Human skeletons were scattered over the floor. Indy guessed that the room was a trap. "Don't touch anything!" he told Shorty.

But Shorty triggered the trap! The roof of the room started to lower and spikes rose up through the floor. Indy and Shorty screamed for Willie to help them. She entered the tunnel, plunged her hand into a gap in the wall and pulled a lever. They were safe... for now.

Indy, Shorty and Willie were deep within an underground temple. It was ruled by the evil Mola Ram, High Priest of an ancient, wicked cult called the Thuggees. Indy and his friends found the Thuggees making a human sacrifice to their god, Kali. Mola Ram removed the sacrificial man's still-beating heart. Then the Thuggees placed the man into a cage and lowered him into a burning pit.

"Have you ever seen anything like this before?" asked Willie.

"Nobody's seen this for a hundred years," Indy replied.

Indy noticed that the Thuggees had three sacred Sankara stones. According to legend, the Sankara stones could grant supernatural powers. The Thuggees were planning to take over the world! Indy took the stones and then heard a child's scream. The village children were there, and they were being forced to work in a mine! But before Indy could do anything, he, Shorty and Willie were taken prisoner. Mola Ram forced Indy to drink the blood of Kali. The blood put him under a spell and turned him into a Thuggee. Indy took part in another ceremony, with Willie as the sacrifice!

"Wake up, Dr Jones!" Shorty yelled, grabbing his hand. Under the spell of Kali, Indy hit the little boy, knocking him to the floor. Shorty stared at Indy with tears of hurt and confusion in his eyes.

"Indy, I love you!" he cried to his hero. "You're my best friend. Wake up!

He grabbed a flaming torch and jabbed Indy in the stomach, shocking him out of the spell!

They fought off the guards and pulled Willie out of the pit. Indy took the sacred stones and dashed into the mine to free the children. Then he jumped into a mine-cart with Shorty and Willie. Within seconds they were hurtling through a network of underground caves! But Mola Ram and his Thuggee guards were hot on their tail.

"We're going too fast!" Willie screamed.

They were about to run out of track when the brake lever had snapped off, so Indy used his feet to slow them down. Then they dashed out of the tunnel and found a long rope bridge over a deep canyon.

Willie and Shorty made their way across the bridge, but Mola Ram and his men were waiting for them! Indy said something to Shorty in Chinese.

"Hang on, lady," Shorty told Willie. "We're going for a ride!"

"Is he nuts?" cried Willie, wrapping her arm in the rope of the bridge.

"He's not nuts," said Shorty confidently. "He's crazy."

Then Indy raised his sword and slashed the main rope of the bridge!

The bridge broke in half and most of the guards fell into the crocodile-infested river below. Shorty and Willie climbed to safety as Mola Ram and Indy tried to pull each other off the bridge.

Suddenly, Indy had an idea. He spoke the ancient words that started the magic of the sacred stones! The stones began to glow until they burned through the bag, and all but one fell into the river. Mola Ram grabbed at them and fell to his death.

The British Army arrived and overpowered the remaining Thuggees. Indy, Willie, Shorty and all the kidnapped children returned to the village and there was a great celebration!

INDY QUEST

CAN YOU SPOT INDY'S POSSESSIONS HIDDEN IN THIS ANCIENT GRAVEYARD?

CODE BREAKER

THE ARMY HAS INTERCEPTED SOME SECRET MESSAGES, BUT THEY'RE IN CODE. CRACK THE CODE TO FIND THE HIDDEN MESSAGES. FILL IN THE CODE BREAKER BELOW AS YOU FIGURE OUT WHAT EACH LETTER STANDS FOR. (SOME HAVE ALREADY BEEN FILLED IN TO HELP YOU OUT.) THEN MAKE UP YOUR OWN SECRET MESSAGES!

VNQQ RTPRKTK SZTNY VCKV CRY JKVCNA CKY FNNT IRPTKBBNP.

VCN NTNWE CKY VKINT VCN KAI.

VCN XCRQPANT CKDN FNNT CRPPNT RT VCN VNWBQN.

ZTQE PA SZTNY XKT YKDN VCN HAKRQ.

VCN XAEYVKQ YIMQQ RY DNAE BZUNAJMQ.

A	B	C	D	E	F	G	H	I	J	K	L	M
K		C										W

N	O	P	Q	R	S	T	U	V	W	X	Y	Z
		O				V				G		L

SHADOW PLAY

Only two of these shadows really belong to Indiana Jones – the others are all impostors! Use your powers of observation to locate the two matching shadows.

WORD SEEKER

A	N	G	C	O	A	D	V	E	N	T	U	R	E	F	L	I	G	N	C
E	I	P	A	U	D	Y	N	K	F	Y	B	L	A	U	D	L	V	I	H
H	S	N	V	D	D	N	V	A	K	C	S	J	C	E	P	F	H	O	J
L	J	P	D	J	T	A	E	H	S	A	K	A	T	O	R	C	N	I	F
D	R	F	S	I	Q	G	R	J	U	K	J	D	A	R	Y	C	A	Q	L
Q	I	T	D	T	A	O	A	Q	D	S	C	I	H	S	G	L	U	D	H
B	V	B	N	U	J	N	H	M	F	K	E	I	P	S	B	F	C	A	G
K	U	I	V	B	Y	G	A	E	J	A	J	P	U	D	F	S	M	R	F
E	A	O	R	P	D	R	I	V	A	I	E	Q	H	Q	T	U	K	J	Q
L	Y	F	O	J	I	G	E	E	R	U	S	A	E	R	T	E	Y	C	J
C	O	L	K	O	B	T	F	N	T	E	Y	L	C	T	J	A	K	U	O
N	A	Q	N	J	J	P	A	T	E	G	B	F	Y	F	V	J	N	I	H
R	F	K	E	U	E	D	C	G	F	V	Y	N	H	L	C	I	F	A	N
I	U	Q	H	D	S	J	H	I	A	J	K	E	B	R	O	J	O	G	B
B	K	L	C	Q	F	P	L	E	C	D	H	R	L	R	N	D	B	V	K
H	J	F	V	H	J	U	A	Q	T	I	E	A	Y	X	Q	K	P	U	G
N	O	P	O	R	A	G	O	L	S	J	F	N	J	O	O	E	S	R	K
G	L	D	D	L	C	U	F	T	K	O	E	B	T	F	S	N	G	E	D
A	K	C	Q	I	J	I	P	B	S	O	T	B	D	V	A	J	Y	P	Q
G	S	N	A	K	E	S	H	F	N	D	K	E	J	G	K	T	D	P	I

- ☐ ADVENTURE
- ☐ AKATOR
- ☐ ARTEFACTS
- ☐ DOVCHENKO
- ☐ INDIANA
- ☐ JUNIOR
- ☐ MARION
- ☐ MUTT
- ☐ OXLEY
- ☐ PERU
- ☐ PSYCHIC
- ☐ QUICKSAND
- ☐ SNAKES
- ☐ SPALKO
- ☐ TREASURE

THE LAST CRUSADE

It was 1938 and Indy had been invited to a meeting with multi-millionaire Walter Donovan. Donovan explained that he had found a wonderful stone tablet. It was the first of three hidden markers that revealed the location of the legendary Holy Grail!

Donovan had hired an expert on the Holy Grail to find it, but the expert had disappeared. At first Indy didn't want to help, but then Donovan told him that the missing expert was Henry Jones Sr, Indy's father!

Indy remembered a package he had received from Venice earlier that day. He opened it and found his father's Grail diary, containing all his research into the legend.

"What's the old fool got himself into now?" asked Indy's friend, Marcus Brody.

"I don't know," said Indy grimly. "But whatever it is, he's in over his head!"

Indy and Marcus travelled to Venice, where Dr Elsa Schneider met them. The Grail diary led them to the ancient tomb,

which was mentioned in the Grail legend. Indy took a rubbing of the engraving on the knight's shield.

"This is it!" he exclaimed. "We found it! The *shield* is the second marker!"

"Just like your father, giddy as a schoolboy!" Elsa laughed.

Meanwhile, Marcus was attacked by a group of men who tried to destroy the tomb by setting it on fire! Indy and the beautiful doctor escaped from the tomb, but the men who attacked Marcus were hot on their trail.

After an incredible boat chase through the canals of Venice, Indy discovered that the men were part of an ancient

order called the Brotherhood of the Cruciform Sword. For hundreds of years, it had been their job to protect the Grail.

Indy's father was being held prisoner in Brunwald Castle in Austria. Indy instructed Marcus to travel to Turkey and meet his old friend Sallah in the city of Iskenderun. Meanwhile, Indy and Elsa travelled to Austria.

Brunwald Castle was occupied by Hitler's Nazi soldiers. Indy sneaked in and broke into the room where his father was being held.

"Junior!" cried Dr Jones Sr.

"Don't call me that!" said Indy through gritted teeth.

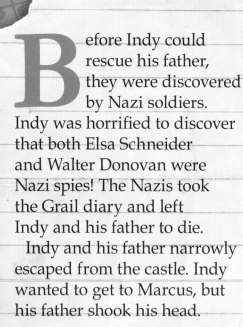

Before Indy could rescue his father, they were discovered by Nazi soldiers. Indy was horrified to discover that both Elsa Schneider and Walter Donovan were Nazi spies! The Nazis took the Grail diary and left Indy and his father to die.

Indy and his father narrowly escaped from the castle. Indy wanted to get to Marcus, but his father shook his head.

"We have to get to Berlin!" he said.

The Grail diary contained instructions for how to survive the final challenge. Without it, they could not save the Grail from the Nazis. They raced to Berlin and rescued the Grail diary from Dr Schneider. Then they travelled to the Republic of Hatay to find Sallah.

Sallah told them that Marcus had been captured – and he had the map showing the location of the Grail! There was no time to lose. The three men managed to find the Nazis and rescue Marcus Brody. Then they set off to find the Grail.

When the four friends arrived in the Canyon of the Crescent Moon, the Nazis were already there – and so were Elsa Schneider and

Walter Donovan! However, the temple entrance was rigged with three booby traps and the Nazis could not get past.

Suddenly, the guards spotted the adventurers and captured them!

"Give Dr Jones some room," said Donovan, pointing his gun at Indy. "He's going to get the Grail for us."

"Shooting me won't get you anywhere," said Indy.

"You're absolutely right," Donovan replied.

He shifted his arm and shot Indy's father!

"The healing power of the Grail is the only thing that can save your father now," Donovan smirked.

Furious but helpless, Indy stepped into the booby-trapped entrance and opened the Grail diary.

The first trap was called the 'Breath of God'.

"Only the penitent man will pass," Indy read aloud.

Just in time, he realised that a penitent man *kneels*. He dropped to his knees as a huge blade flew past his face.

The second trap was called 'Proceed in the Footsteps of the Word'. The floor was covered in lettered tiles. Indy spelled out the name of God and safely crossed the unstable floor.

The third and final trap was called the 'Path of God'. Indy reached an opening in the side of a sheer cliff face. There seemed to be no way to cross the gap. This required a leap of faith. Closing his eyes, Indy stepped out into the chasm... and his foot landed on something firm. It was an illusion! There *was* a footpath across the gap, but it was almost impossible to see.

Indy hurried across the bridge and found a knight kneeling at a table in a cave. He had been there for seven hundred years, guarding the Grail. The cave walls were lined with chalices. Before Indy could explain anything, Donovan and Dr Schneider arrived.

"Which one is it?" demanded Donovan, staring at the many chalices.

"You must choose," said the knight. "But choose wisely. "The true Grail will bring you life... the false Grail will take it from you."

"Let me choose," said Dr Schneider.

She picked an ornate chalice, made of gold and encrusted with jewels. Donovan drank from it and his face contorted. Then his body decayed and turned to dust.

Dr Schneider had known that the chalice would not be made from gold. She had turned her back on the Nazis. Indy picked up a simple earthenware jug.

"*That's* the cup of a carpenter," he said.

Indy drank from the chalice, and nothing happened. He had chosen the true Grail! Indy and Dr Schneider ran back and Indy's father drank from the chalice. He then poured the holy water on to his father's wound, which healed instantly.

Dr Schneider tried to leave the temple with the chalice, but the building began to collapse around her. Dr Schneider died trying to rescue the Grail. Glory and power meant more to her than her own life. But Indy, Dr Jones, Sallah and Marcus escaped, ready for their next adventure!

DOOR HANGER

OFTEN YOU WILL NEED PEACE AND QUIET WHILE YOU ARE DECODING SECRET MESSAGES OR TRAINING FOR YOUR NEXT ADVENTURE. THIS DOOR HANGER WILL TELL YOUR FAMILY WHETHER THEY CAN DISTURB YOU OR NOT!

Trace or copy the design opposite onto a piece of white card.

Trim the card to the right shape.

Trace the other side of the hanger on to the other side of the card.

Colour it in! Make sure you get all the colours right.

Place the hanger over your bedroom doorknob to show whether you want visitors or not.

You can use this design to make exciting door hangers for all your friends and family!

U.S. ARMY
1B7731
OFFICIAL USE ONLY

PART ONE

THE KINGDOM
OF THE CRYSTAL SKULL

1957 On a long, empty stretch of Nevada's state highway, a convoy of army vehicles headed towards a restricted army base.

The convoy reached a gate topped with barbed wire. Three soldiers stepped forward and waved for the convoy to stop. A colonel got out of the staff car. He was a tall, hard-faced man. The soldiers saluted him.

"Sorry, gentlemen, but this entire area is off-limits for the next twenty-four hours for weapons testing," said the sergeant. "That applies to you, too, Colonel."

The colonel just kept walking forwards as three soldiers leaped from the truck and shot down the guards with automatic rifles.

Quickly and efficiently, the three fake guards took the places of the dead men. The gate slid open and the convoy set off again. It headed towards a massive building that looked like an aeroplane hangar.

The convoy stopped in front of the huge hangar doors. Two soldiers opened the trunk of the staff car and pulled out two blindfolded men. One of them was in his fifties, overweight, bruised and battered. The other man was Indiana Jones.

Indy had been on an archaeological dig in Mexico when he was kidnapped in the middle of the night. Since then he had been tied up, punched, gagged and stuffed into various vehicles. His friend Mac had been taken at the same time, and Indy still had no idea who had taken them – or why.

His captors removed his blindfold and Indy heard them talking in Russian.

"Ruskies!" Mac said under his breath. "This won't be easy."

"Not as easy as it used to be," Indy agreed.

The man who was dressed as an American colonel glared at Indy.

"You recognise this building?" he asked. "Go to hell," Indy said. The man punched Indy once, but a sudden shout stopped him from doing it again. A tall, pale woman walked towards them. A sword hung at her side.

"At ease, Antonin Dovchenko," the woman said, turning to Indy. "I am Dr Irina Spalko. Three times I have received the Order of Lenin, also a medal as a Hero of Socialist Labour. And why? Because I intuit things. I know them before anyone else, and what I do not know, I learn."

She tapped her finger on Indy's head. "And what I need to know now is in here."

The doors rolled open and the hangar was filled with stacks of wooden packing crates and metal shipping containers. There were boxes of every size and shape, barrels filled with machine parts, stuffed paper bags, bulging briefcases and many other things that Indy could not even identify.

"This is where your government hides its military treasures," Spalko said. "Object we seek: rectangular storage container. Dimensions: two metres by one metre by two hundred centimetres. Contents of box are highly magnetised. The crate is no doubt familiar to you."

"I have no idea what you're talking about," said Indy.

Spalko pressed the tip of her sword against Indy's throat.

"Killing me isn't going to solve your problem," he told her.

When Spalko realised that threatening Indy's life would not make him talk, she turned her attention to Mac, ordering one of her men to gun him down.

"I say once more, Dr Jones, you *will* help us locate the container!" she snapped.

Indy had to give in. He could not let his friend die.

"Highly magnetised, right?" he said. "We need to look for signs of the magnetic field."

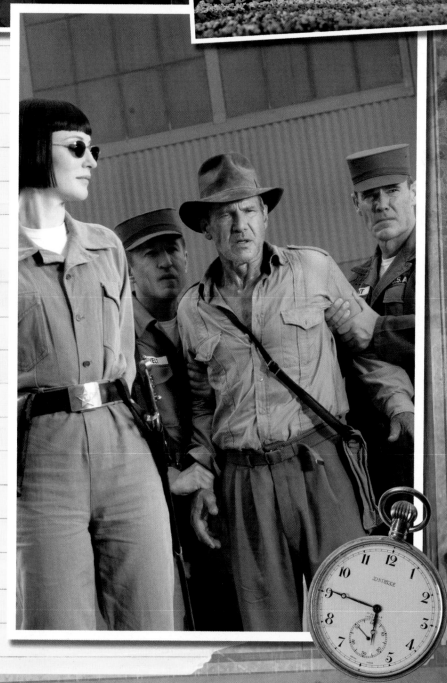

Although he hated doing it, Indy helped his attackers to find the crate they were seeking. It was so magnetic that the hands of the Russians' wristwatches spun madly. Spalko pried the lid open. Inside was a stainless-steel coffin and a metallic body bag. It was labelled 'Roswell'.

While the Russians were distracted by the crate, Indy grabbed his whip from the soldier guarding him. He disarmed him, took his rifle, and tossed another gun to Mac. Then he aimed his gun at Spalko. "Guns down or she's dead!" he ordered.

But Spalko just smiled. Feeling sick, Indy turned to see Mac pointing the gun at his head.

He couldn't believe it. His friend had betrayed him.

"Drop the gun," Dovchenko said.

Indy slammed his rifle down and it spluttered bullets in all directions. One bullet hit a soldier and he screamed, his finger pressing on the trigger of his gun. Bullets spat into the air, and Indy dove towards the nearest crates.

Indy leaped between crates, dodging bullets, as Spalko put the Roswell crate into the back of a jeep. He used his whip to swing himself into the vehicle behind Spalko's, tossing the driver out and taking the steering wheel. Indy used the jeep as a weapon to batter Spalko's, sending it crashing into a stack of crates. Spalko flew over the bonnet and Indy raced away in her jeep!

Seconds later, the staff car bore down on him from the front and a truck was coming from behind. Indy flicked his whip around one of the beams and hoisted himself straight out of the jeep. Below him, the three vehicles collided and crashed into stacks of crates. Several crates burst open and Indy saw a gleam of gold inside one of them. It was the Ark of the Covenant!

"So *this* is where it ended up," he muttered.

Indy raced for the exit as bullets whizzed around his ears. Suddenly another jeep drove into him, and he smashed through the windscreen. It was Dovchenko! The Russian could not see with Indy in the way, and he drove down concrete steps and crashed into a wall.

They found themselves in an underground bunker. Indy could see a railway flat car, a jet engine fastened to it, at the start of a set of train tracks. The tracks led into a dark tunnel. Dovchenko hurled Indy into the engine's control panel, activating a flashing red light. A hum of immense power grew louder and louder as he squashed Indy against the side of the jet engine, choking him.

Twisting his head around, Indy saw the jet engine's throttle. He stuck out his leg and kicked it. With a deafening roar, the engine sent the flat car streaking down the tunnel, with Indy and Dovchenko clinging to it!

The flat car tore down the railway tracks at two hundred miles an hour. Indy and Dovchenko could only cling on for dear life, hoping that they wouldn't be melted by the scorching heat of the engine.

Suddenly the engine quietened from a scream to a soft hum. The flat car slowed, the engine shut down, and the strange vehicle stopped at the end of the tracks.

Dovchenko collapsed and Indy rolled on to the ground, feeling dizzy, as if he had been in a boxing match. He looked back in the direction of the warehouse and saw a convoy of vehicles heading towards him. It was the Russians. Indy knew that he had to escape before they got any closer. He could see a ridge of hills in the distance and started walking that way, ignoring the shaking in his legs.

After walking for what felt like hours, Indy saw a town. He could hardly believe his luck at finding it in the middle of the desert like this. It was a strangely perfect town, with neat little streets, smart new homes and tidy, manicured gardens. Indy thought that it was a little odd to find a town out here in the middle of nowhere, but he wasn't going to worry about that.

Suddenly Indy spotted a military jeep heading his way, packed with Russian soldiers! He dashed in through the back door of the nearest house.

"Anyone home?" he called out. He heard a sound from the living room and found a family watching television.

"Russian spies!" he cried. "Here, in your town!"

None of them turned around.

"What's wrong with you people?" Indy bellowed.

He grabbed the father's arm, but to his horror he pulled it *completely off!*

Indy could hardly believe his eyes. They were mannequins! Then he jumped as he heard a wailing siren.

"That's not just any siren..." he realised.

He ran out through the front door. He could see a mannequin postman standing at the mailbox. On the other side of the street, a mannequin ice-cream man was selling ice cream to mannequin children. The siren was still blaring at top volume.

"Oh, this isn't good," Indy said, starting to panic. "This isn't good at all!"

He had walked into a nuclear testing site... and they were about to detonate a bomb!

A voice suddenly blared from hidden loudspeakers.

"Detonation commencing in T-minus one minute."

Indy ran down the street, desperate to escape, but then bullets peppered the ground at his feet. The Russians had found him!

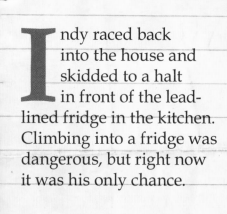

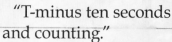

Indy raced back into the house and skidded to a halt in front of the lead-lined fridge in the kitchen. Climbing into a fridge was dangerous, but right now it was his only chance.

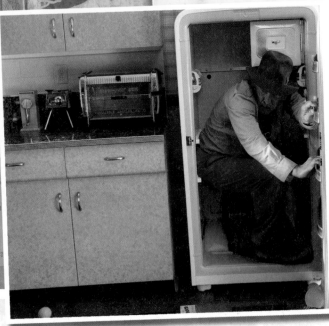

"T-minus ten seconds and counting."

Indy emptied the fridge and crammed himself inside, slamming the door.

"Any fallout shelter in a storm," he said.

A split second later, the dark sky was lit up by a white glare. Then a nuclear explosion came out of the sky, flattening out as it hit the ground. The little town was devastated. Houses were destroyed in seconds and the mannequins melted.

A white fridge flew through the air and landed with a loud thump, rolling over and over on the soft ground far from the town. Finally the door opened and Indy staggered out. He was dizzy, bruised and bewildered... but he was alive.

Indy was rescued by an Army patrol, decontaminated and then interrogated by the FBI. He told them that the Russians kidnapped him and that Mac was a spy, but the FBI agents were suspicious. The way they saw it, Indy had helped the Russians break into a top-secret military installation and steal something very important. Despite his impressive war record, they thought that he might be a spy too.

"What was inside the steel container?" Indy asked, remembering that it had said 'Roswell' on the side. "Remains of a spaceman?"

"Hangar 51 is merely a storage facility for aircraft components," said one of the FBI agents.

"Sure it is," Indy fumed. "What exactly am I being charged with, other than surviving a nuclear bomb?"

"Nothing... yet," the agent said. "But your close association with George McHale calls into question all your activities, including some of your actions during the war. Let's say for now that you are a person of interest to the Bureau."

A few days later, Indy was in the middle of teaching a class when the door opened and Dean Stanforth appeared.

"May I have a moment, professor?" Stanforth said.

Indy walked out of the classroom into the corridor.

"FBI agents showed up this morning," said Stanforth. "They ransacked your office."

"And you let them?" Indy bellowed.

"They had search warrants," said Stanforth. "The university can't afford to become involved in this."

"So you're firing me?" said Indy.

"You're not being fired, exactly," Stanforth replied. "An indefinite leave of absence. You'll continue to receive your full salary for –"

"I don't want their money," Indy snapped.

"Be reasonable," Stanforth pleaded. "You don't know what I had to go through to get that much for you."

"What you went through?" Indy laughed bitterly. "What exactly did *you* have to go through, Charlie?"

Stanforth looked at him sadly.

"I resigned," he said.

Indy decided to catch a train to New York and travel overnight to London. Then he would look for work in Europe. He felt worn out. The last two years had been very difficult. Both his father and his friend Marcus Brody had died, and now Mac had betrayed him.

The next day, Indy arrived at the station and pushed through the crowd of people on the platform. He stepped into a carriage, but he didn't notice two large men in dark suits who followed him on board. The whistle blew and the train slowly moved forwards.

At that moment Indy saw a young man on a Harley-Davidson. He zoomed along the platform beside the train and yelling up at the carriage.

"Hey, professor!" he bellowed. "You're an old friend of Harold Oxley, right?"

"What about him?" asked Indy.

"They're gonna kill him!" the lad yelled.

The young man took Indy over the road to Arnie's Diner. It was packed with university students and townies with leather jackets and ducktail haircuts.

"Ox and I haven't spoken in twenty years," Indy said. "He cut me off, angry about something. He never told me why. But I miss him. He was a brilliant guy. Even if he could talk you to sleep once he got going on a topic."

The biker grinned.

"When I was a kid, that's exactly how I got to sleep," he said. "The Ox was better than warm milk. I'm Mutt Williams."

"Are you related to Ox?" Indy asked.

"I always thought of him as my uncle, even though he isn't." Mutt said. "My dad died in the war. Six months ago Ox wrote to Mum from Peru. He'd found a crystal skull, like the one Mitchell-Hedges found."

"How do you know about the Mitchell-Hedges skull?" Indy enquired.

"Ox told me," said Mutt. "He said that the skull has psychic powers. He said he was taking it to a place called Akator."

"If you believe the stories, Akator is a lost city," said Indy. "The legend is that a native tribe called the Ugha built a city of solid gold with the help of the gods. They invented technology that was thousands of years ahead of its time. In 1546, a conquistador named Francesco de Orellana –known as the Gilded Man, because of his love of gold – disappeared in the Amazon looking for Akator."

"Even if Akator exists, why would Ox want to take the crystal skull there?" Mutt asked.

"Some say that a crystal skull was stolen from Akator when Orellana was looking for the place. It's believed that whoever finds the missing skull and returns it to Akator's temple will be granted control over its power."

"Power? What kind of power?" Mutt asked.

"I don't know, kid," Indy said. "It's just a *story*."

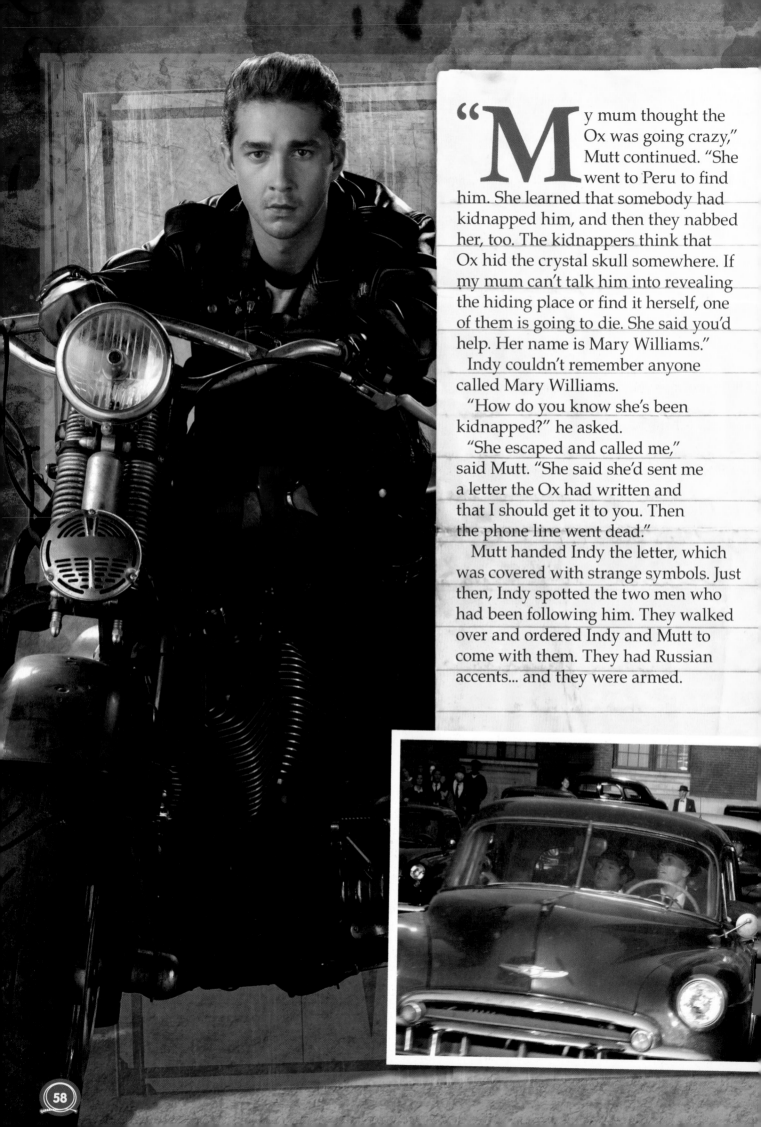

"My mum thought the Ox was going crazy," Mutt continued. "She went to Peru to find him. She learned that somebody had kidnapped him, and then they nabbed her, too. The kidnappers think that Ox hid the crystal skull somewhere. If my mum can't talk him into revealing the hiding place or find it herself, one of them is going to die. She said you'd help. Her name is Mary Williams."

Indy couldn't remember anyone called Mary Williams.

"How do you know she's been kidnapped?" he asked.

"She escaped and called me," said Mutt. "She said she'd sent me a letter the Ox had written and that I should get it to you. Then the phone line went dead."

Mutt handed Indy the letter, which was covered with strange symbols. Just then, Indy spotted the two men who had been following him. They walked over and ordered Indy and Mutt to come with them. They had Russian accents... and they were armed.

Indy and Mutt walked towards the exit between the Russian agents. Just as Mutt was about to pass a university student who stood near a group of hoodlums, Indy whispered to him.

"Mutt," he said, "punch the prep in the face."

Mutt was quick to obey! He hit the boy and angry shouts rang out from all sides. Mutt had started a brawl!

Indy and Mutt charged towards the door. Behind them, the chaos held the Russian agents back. Indy and Mutt ran into the side alley where Mutt had parked his motorbike.

"You sure you're old enough to handle this thing?" Indy asked, climbing on board.

Mutt looked over his shoulder.

"The question you should be asking yourself is whether you're young enough to hang on!" he said with a grin.

Indy thought hard. He guessed that Irina Spalko must have captured Oxley, but not before he had hidden the skull. Spalko had allowed Oxley to pass a secret message to Mary Williams, certain that the message would eventually reach Indy.

Just then a black car skidded to a stop in front of them. Mutt drove his bike forward, skidded past them and zoomed down the street. A second car chased after them. It pulled up beside Mutt, and then someone reached through the car's back window. They pulled Indy off the bike and into the back of the car!

Indy punched one Russian in the nose and crawled over the second towards the opposite window. Mutt rode around to the other side of the car as Indy slithered out of the window and pulled himself back on to the bike!

Up ahead, another car joined
the chase. Mutt swerved and
drove into the town library!
Students ran out of the way
and books flew into the air
as Mutt raced through the
library and out the other side.

They rode out into a traffic
jam as one of the Russians'
sedans came into view. Mutt
headed for the town square,
weaving through the cars.
The jam was caused by a
group of marchers waving
placards and chanting
slogans. Mutt rode the bike
right into the march!

The Russians' car rode
up on to the pavement and
followed them into the heart
of the demonstration, sending
protestors and placards
flying in all directions. A
placard landed on the car
windscreen. Unable to see
where he was going, the
driver crashed into a statue.
Indy and Mutt roared away.
They were safe... for now.

At Indy's home, Indy compared the symbols in Oxley's letter with those in one of his books.

"I thought so," he said at last. "Koihoma. An obscure language. Ox, you clever devil!"

He began to scribble some notes on a notepad. Mutt watched him thoughtfully.

"You know, for an old guy, you ain't bad in a fight," he said.

"Thanks a bunch, kid," Indy said. "Partial transcription of Ox's letter. He wrote, 'Follow the lines in the earth only gods can read to Orellana's cradle, guarded by the living dead'."

"Orellana," Mutt said. "The gilded conquistador, right?"

"But what could Ox mean?" Indy asked himself. "Of course! He means the Nazca Lines!"

Indy explained that the Nazca lines are etched into the desert floor in Peru. They can only be seen from the air.

"You get it?" he exclaimed. "Only gods can read them because the gods reside in the sky! The crystal skull is somewhere in Nazca, Peru!"

A couple of days later, Mutt and Indy landed in Nazca, Peru. Mutt had visited many places in Europe, but Peru was very different. The desert town was full of tiny, white buildings with red roofs. It was a poor, rough town, populated by stray animals, peasants and dangerous-looking travellers. The streets bustled with people selling strange-looking food and Mutt felt as if he had stepped into another world.

At last, Indy managed to track down someone who remembered Oxley.

"A couple of months back he came staggering into town, ranting like a wild man," Indy told Mutt. "The police took him to the sanitarium."

"Your parents must have had a cow," said Mutt. "My mum and I weren't on the best of terms when she came down here looking for Ox. She got annoyed because I quit school."

"Why's that?" Indy asked.

"All they do is teach you chess, debate, fencing," said Mutt. "I can handle a blade like nobody's business. But what a waste of time."

"So instead of attending school, you work?" asked Indy.

"Mechanic work," said Mutt, nodding. "Mostly repairing motorbikes."

"Plan on doing that forever?" said Indy.

"Maybe I do, man,' Mutt snapped. "Anything wrong with that?"

Indy smiled.

"Not a thing, kid," he said. "And don't let anybody tell you different."

As they walked towards the sanitarium, Mutt asked Indy how he learned the Peruvian's local language. When the boy heard that Indy had learned it while in Pancho Villa's army, he was surprised and impressed. Pancho Villa was a famous Mexican revolutionary general.

The sanitarium was part of an old monastery, and a nun let them in.

"We're looking for Harold Oxley," Indy explained.

"I remember him," the nun said. "He was here a couple of months ago, but

men came and stole him away. Men with guns."

"Sister, could you perhaps show us the room where he was confined?" Indy asked.

The nun led Indy and Mutt down a dirty corridor, which was lined with cells. Mutt could see men and women dressed in rags, some of them wailing and screaming, others crouching quietly in the dark.

Suddenly, one inmate reached through the bars and grabbed Mutt by the collar of his motorcycle jacket. He could not get free! Then a strong pair of hands grabbed him from behind and pulled him free. "Try to keep up," Indy said calmly.

"Sister Mara says that Oxley was deranged," Indy told Mutt. "He drew pictures all over the walls of his cell."

He took out Oxley's letter.

"'The lines only gods can read'," Indy read aloud. "That much we know. But Ox writes, 'to Orellana's cradle'. It doesn't make sense. Francisco de Orellana wasn't born in Peru. He entered the jungle to search for El Dorado. He and his six lieutenants were never heard from again. So how could the Nazca Lines lead to Orellana's 'cradle'?"

Mutt didn't have an answer. Sister Mara opened one of the cells and Indy and Mutt walked inside.

The poor little room contained an old bed, a dirty sink and a wooden bucket. The floor was covered with sand, but Mutt gasped when he saw what was on the stone walls. They were covered with words and drawings of strangely shaped skulls of every size.

"Ox, man, what happened to you?" Mutt murmured, his heart aching for his friend.

Indy was looking at the words Oxley had scratched on the walls.

"Every word here – in Spanish, Italian, French, Arabic – means 'return'," said Indy.

"Return where?" asked Mutt.

"Or return *what*?" Indy said, looking at the strange, long skulls. "In pre-Columbian cultures, a baby's head would be sandwiched between two boards to force it to grow into a longer shape."

Suddenly Indy spotted something beneath the sand on the floor.

"Ox etched a drawing into the floor!" he cried, sweeping away the sand.

"What is it?" Mutt demanded.

"Gravestones," Indy said, looking down at the drawing. "Some sort of sacred burial ground."

"A cemetery," said Mutt. "But what does it mean?"

"It means that Ox didn't mean us to take him literally when he wrote 'cradle'," Indy said with a grin. "He was referring to Orellana's grave – in that cemetery."

"But didn't you say that Orellana had vanished without a trace?" Mutt asked.

Indy nodded, his eyes gleaming.

"It looks like Oxley found him," he explained.

L ightning was flashing when Mutt and Indy drove up to Chauchilla Cemetery, on a hillside high above the Nazca lines. They entered the cemetery through a creaking iron gate. Mutt was feeling very nervous.

"How old is this place?" he asked.

"A thousand years old, at least," said Indy.

They walked between two twisted old trees. If they had looked up, they might have seen two figures slipping down from the branches and slinking into the shadows. But they were too busy looking at the graves around them. Many of the graves had been robbed. Human skeletons were lying about everywhere.

"Just *what* are we supposed to be looking for?" Mutt asked.

"Orellana's grave won't be above ground," said Indy. "It'll be underground, or inside a burial mound. You'll be needing this."

He handed Mutt one of the spades. Something moved nearby and Mutt whirled around.

"You're jumping at shadows," said Indy. There's nothing here but a bunch of –"

Before Indy could say another word, something sprang at him, knocking him down. Mutt fell backwards into a skeleton, which came to life and grabbed him!

Mutt pushed his attacker away and saw that he was wearing a mask of bones. He had stripes painted on his chest to look like ribs. Then Indy's fist shattered the skeleton mask and the man raced away before they could catch him. Indy ducked, but Mutt was knocked off his feet into an open grave by another attacker!

Suddenly Mutt saw a warrior above him with a blowgun held to his lips. Mutt threw his knife into the warrior's shoulder, but instantly a second warrior appeared with another blowgun. Mutt was defenceless!

Then a hand clamped itself over the tube. Indy blew down the other end of the weapon and the dart slammed into the back of the warrior's throat. He dropped the blowgun and collapsed.

The first warrior pulled Mutt's blade from his shoulder and lunged at the boy, but Indy was ready for him. He flicked the knife away with his whip, and sent the warrior scurrying into the shadows. Mutt stared at Indy in absolute amazement.

"You're a *teacher*?" he said in awe.

"Part time," Indy replied.

Indy helped the boy out of the tomb.
"Man, who were those guys?" asked Mutt.

"Custodians," Indy said. "Descendants
of the Nazca warriors. Ox wasn't kidding
when he wrote that Orellana's cradle
was guarded by 'the living dead'."

Indy led them to the edge of the
cemetery, where they found a stone wall
full of small gaps. There were skulls and
piles of bones in the gaps, but no tomb.

"Dead end?" Mutt asked.

Indy stuck his fingers into one of
the skulls' eye sockets and pulled on
the rope he found inside. The stone
wall opened up and showed them a
narrow corridor. In silent wonder, Mutt
followed Indy into the corridor. They
walked down a long flight of steps, past
skeletons with strangely shaped skulls.

"Like the one Ox drew," Mutt said.

They clambered through tunnels and at
last found themselves in a small chamber.

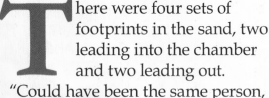

There were four sets of footprints in the sand, two leading into the chamber and two leading out.

"Could have been the same person, twice," Mutt remarked.

"Not bad, kid," Indy said.

In the chamber were several large shapes wrapped in a strange silver material. Indy opened the many-layered wrappings of the nearest bundle. Eventually he discovered the body of a conquistador. The body was dressed in armour and must have been hundreds of years old. Indy gasped and counted the cocoons.

"Seven!" he cried. "It's Orellana and his men!"

"Here's one that's already been opened!" Mutt called.

Inside the open cocoon, a golden mask covered the face of the conquistador.

"The Gilded Man," Indy said. "Francisco de Orellana himself."

He pulled the body forward and his hands felt a second skull behind it... a crystal skull.

"This isn't possible, not even with today's technology," Indy said in awe. "It's nothing like any skull I've ever seen."

"But why is it *here*?" Mutt asked.

Indy shrugged. "Ox must have found it here and returned it for some reason before he headed for Akator."

As Indy stared at the skull, its huge eyes began to glow with a strange light. Indy found that he couldn't look away. Behind him, Mutt was also hypnotised.

Suddenly there was a crackling, crumbling sound. The floor of the crypt was collapsing! The sound broke the spell of the skull. Just in time, Indy saved Mutt and the skull from falling hundreds of feet below. Grabbing the skull, he pulled Mutt back the way they had come, just ahead of the collapsing floor.

As they staggered out of the burial chamber, they saw dawn breaking. Indy brushed dust from his clothes, and then looked up. His face grew pale and grim.

"Hello, old pal," said a familiar voice.

Mac was standing there, surrounded by armed Russian soldiers. And he was grinning.

END OF PART ONE.
THIS STORY CONTINUES ON PAGE 78

73

SPOT THE DIFFERENCE

A SUCCESSFUL EXPLORER NEEDS TO BE INCREDIBLY OBSERVANT. THESE TWO PICTURES LOOK THE SAME, BUT THERE ARE TEN DIFFERENCES BETWEEN THEM. CAN YOU FIND THEM ALL?

JONES JOKES

INDY ALWAYS HAS A WITTY REMARK, JOKE OR PUN TO HELP HIM AND HIS FRIENDS THROUGH DANGEROUS SITUATIONS. LEARN THESE JOKES TO KEEP YOUR SPIRITS UP WHEN YOU'RE ON YOUR NEXT ADVENTURE!

HOW MANY EGYPTIANS DOES IT TAKE TO CHANGE A LIGHT BULB?

NONE. THEY GET THEIR MUMMIES TO DO IT FOR THEM!

WHAT DO YOU CALL A MAN WITH AN ALLIGATOR UNDER EACH ARM?

ANYTHING HE TELLS YOU TO!

WHAT'S GREY, HAS BIG EARS AND A TRUNK?

A MOUSE ON HOLIDAY!

WHAT'S BLACK AND WHITE AND BLACK AND WHITE AND BLACK AND WHITE?

A PENGUIN ROLLING DOWN A HILL!

WHAT'S GREY AND SQUIRTS JAM AT YOU?

AN ELEPHANT EATING A DOUGHNUT!

WHERE DO DINOSAURS WEAR TIES?

AROUND THEIR TYRANNOSAURUS NECKS!

WHAT HAS A BOTTOM AT THE TOP?

YOUR LEGS!

WHAT'S GREEN AND HANGS IN CAVES?

A POORLY BAT!

WHAT DO YOU CALL A MAN WITH AN ELEPHANT ON HIS HEAD?

AN AMBULANCE!

WHAT'S BROWN AND STICKY?

A STICK!

PART TWO

THE KINGDOM OF THE CRYSTAL SKULL

Indy blinked and tried to get his bearings. He was inside a large tent that was lit by a lantern, tied to a chair. The air was hot and heavy. He realised that he was in the middle of the Amazon jungle. Then he saw Mac sitting opposite him.

"Tell me something, Mac," Indy said. "After the war, how many names did you give the Reds? How many good men died because of you?"

"I don't think you're seeing the big picture, mate," said Mac.

Indy glared at the man who had once been his friend.

"Eventually these ropes are coming off," he said, "and when they do the first thing I'm going to do is break your nose, *comrade*."

"Indy, do you actually believe I care about these Reds?" Mac asked with a laugh. "Or uniforms of any sort?"

"The only thing you care about is money," Indy said.

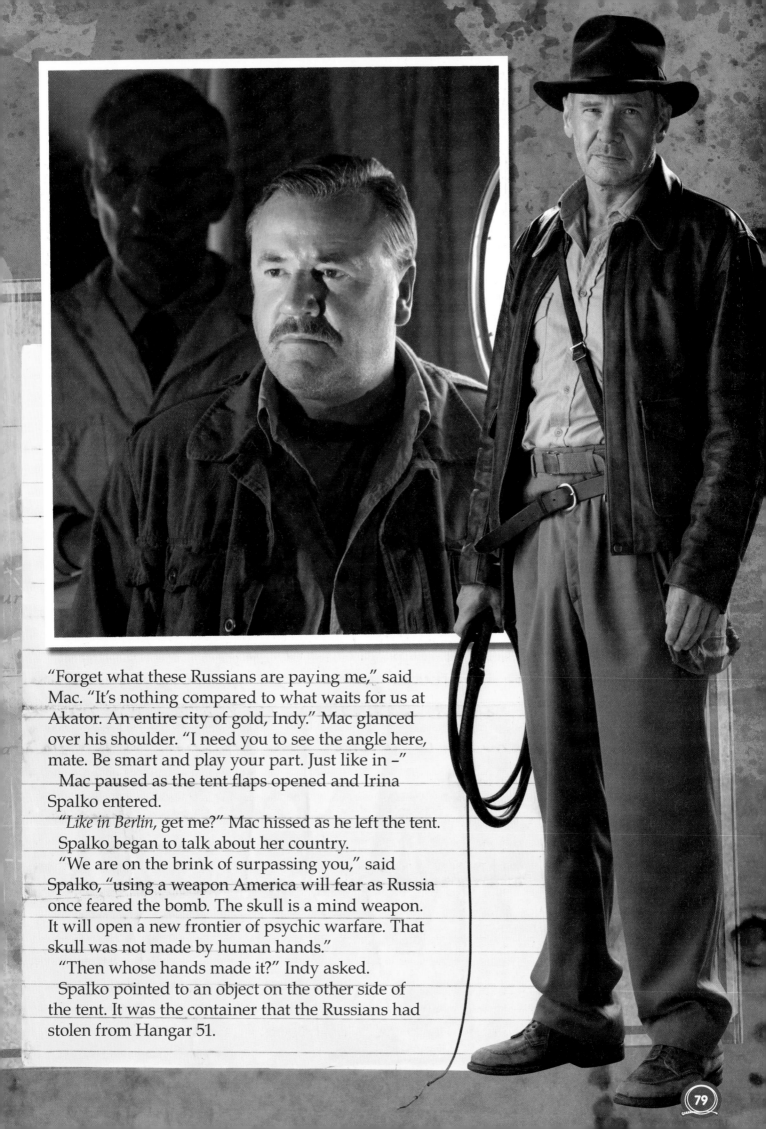

"Forget what these Russians are paying me," said Mac. "It's nothing compared to what waits for us at Akator. An entire city of gold, Indy." Mac glanced over his shoulder. "I need you to see the angle here, mate. Be smart and play your part. Just like in –"

Mac paused as the tent flaps opened and Irina Spalko entered.

"*Like in Berlin*, get me?" Mac hissed as he left the tent.

Spalko began to talk about her country.

"We are on the brink of surpassing you," said Spalko, "using a weapon America will fear as Russia once feared the bomb. The skull is a mind weapon. It will open a new frontier of psychic warfare. That skull was not made by human hands."

"Then whose hands made it?" Indy asked.

Spalko pointed to an object on the other side of the tent. It was the container that the Russians had stolen from Hangar 51.

"The body we liberated from your warehouse wasn't the first we had seen," said Spalko. "We had already dissected two others from crash sites in the Soviet Union."

"Saucer men from Mars?" Indy said scornfully.

"The legends about Akator are true, Dr Jones," said Spalko. "It was a city of supreme beings, with technologies and paranormal abilities."

"You've got to be kidding me," Indy retorted.

"The skull was stolen from Akator in the fifteenth century," Spalko continued. "Whoever returns it –"

"Gets control over its power," Indy interrupted. "I've heard that bedtime story too. But what if Akator doesn't exist?'

Spalko smiled. "You should ask your friend that question. We're certain Professor Oxley has been there."

Indy was taken out of the tent and led towards a figure dancing around one of the campfires. Indy's jaw dropped. It was Oxley. His greying hair was long and stringy and his red-rimmed eyes shone madly in the firelight.

"Ox, it's me!" called Indy. "You remember me, don't you, pal?"

Oxley stopped dancing.

"Through eyes that last I saw in tears," he said. "Through eyes that last I saw in tears..."

Oxley's right hand was twitching.

"Listen to me," Indy said in a firmer voice. "You're Harold Oxley. You were born in Leeds and you were never half this interesting. You and I attended the University of Chicago together. One of our professors was named Ravenwood. Remember? I'm Indy... Henry Jones. No way you could forget me, right?"

But Oxley started dancing again, muttering to himself. Indy turned to Spalko and Mac in a fury.

"What did you do to him?" he demanded.

"We didn't do a thing," Mac said. "It was that skull."

"He will lead us to Akator," said Spalko. "However, we need someone to interpret him for us. Oxley's mind is quite weak. Let's hope that yours is stronger."

They strapped Indy into a chair and put the crystal skull opposite him.

"The crystal structure stimulates the human brain, opening a psychic channel," Spalko said. "Professor Oxley stared too long into its eyes and went mad. I want you to go just mad enough to communicate with him."

Indy's thoughts were silenced by a sudden brightness in the skull's eyes. He could not look away.

"There could be hundreds of such skulls at Akator," Spalko was saying. "Whoever finds them will have power over the mind of every human being."

The light in the skull's eyes seemed to grow stronger. Indy's pulse was throbbing.

"This skull is a destroyer of worlds, Dr Jones – *your* world," Spalko said. "There will be no 'us and them'. Only *us*."

Indy could not reply. The skull had hypnotised him. He was shaking and there was blood on his face,

"That's enough!" Mac yelled. "We'll never find Akator if he dies!"

One of the soldiers covered the skull and Indy blinked, but his face was blank.

"He's under the spell of the skull," Spalko said.

Dovchenko undid Indy's straps and then Indy punched Mac and broke his nose.

"You can't say I didn't warn you," Indy snarled.

"You will speak with Dr Oxley," shrieked Spalko. "You will lead us to Akator."

"I'd sooner lead you to hell," Indy replied.

Indy was pulled out of the tent. From a separate tent, two soldiers dragged Mutt out into the night. Spalko pulled out her sword and pointed it at the boy.

"Don't give these Reds a thing," Mutt told Indy.

"You heard him," Indy told Spalko.

But then a woman was dragged out, yelling and struggling. Indy's mouth dropped open. He would know that voice anywhere. It was Marion Ravenwood.

Oceana

"**W**ell, it's about time you showed up, Jones," Marion snapped.

"Mum!" Mutt cried.

Indy looked even more amazed, if that were possible.

"*Mum*?" he repeated. "*Marion Ravenwood is your mother?*"

"For crying out loud, Jones, is it so hard to figure out?" Marion yelled.

Indy stared at her. "I just... didn't think you'd..."

"Didn't think I'd what – have a life after you left me?"

Indy shook his head. "That's not what I –"

"I've had a pretty good life, Jones," she said. "A darn good life, in fact."

Indy started to feel irritated. Marion was as much of a spitfire as ever.

"Oh, yeah?" he retorted. "Well, so have I."

"Oh, I don't doubt that," Marion said, grinning. "You still leaving a trail of human wreckage in your wake, or have you retired from womanising?"

Indy glared at her. "Why, you looking for a date?"

Spalko threatened Marion with her sword.

"Perhaps you will help us now, Dr Jones," she said.

Indy sat down opposite Oxley.

"To lay their just hands on that Golden Key," Ox said, "that opens the Palace of Eternity." It was a quote from Milton.

"I need you to tell me how to get to Akator," said Indy desperately. "You remember Abner Ravenwood? If you don't tell me how to reach Akator, these people are going to kill his daughter, Marion!"

Oxley's hand was twitching, but the right words failed him. Indy watched Oxley's hand, suddenly realising the truth. Oxley was trying to write something!

"Somebody get me a pen and some paper!" he yelled.

As soon as Oxley had a pen and paper, he started to write in symbols. Indy quickly translated their meaning, and realised that they were directions. With the help of a map, he worked out that they had to follow the River Sono to where it joined the Amazon.

While everyone was distracted, Mutt moved to one end of the table and gripped the edge. Spalko and Dovchenko were leaning over the map. Mutt waited until their faces were right over the other end of the table. Then he picked up the table and hurled it at the two Russians!

Indy, Mutt, Marion and Oxley raced into the dark jungle. The prickly leaves ripped their clothes to shreds. Finally they reached a clearing and stopped. They could hear Russian soldiers searching for them.

"Not that I don't appreciate what you did back there," Indy said, "but we're in unknown territory."

"Well, somebody had to do something," said Mutt. "At least I came up with a plan!"

"This is intolerable," Indy muttered, glaring at him.

Just then, Marion felt the ground go spongy under her feet.

"Don't move!" Indy shouted. "Stay right where you are."

Marion and Indy were thigh deep in a dry sand pit!

"Gently raise your arms over your head," said Indy.

"I'll find something we can use to pull you out!" Mutt cried, rushing off into the forest.

"Ox," Indy said, "are you going to help us?"

"Help?" said Oxley. He turned and walked off.

Marion gazed at Indy, realising that if she was going to tell him the truth it could be now or never.

"About Mutt, Indy," Marion said. "He's –"

"A good kid. I know. You should probably get off his back about completing school."

"Indy –"

"I mean, not everyone's cut out for it."

"His... his name is Henry," Marion went on.

Marion took a breath.

"He's your son!" she said.

I ndy gaped at Marion. "Why the hell didn't you make him finish school?" he yelled. Before Marion could reply, something long and heavy thumped down between her and Indy. Mutt had returned.

"Grab hold of it!" Mutt shouted. "I'll pull you out!"

Marion held on and Mutt pulled her out. The thing was round and cold, and she wasn't surprised when Indy screamed. He had always been terrified of snakes.

"Just grab it, Indy!" Marion said.

"It's a *snake*! And it's hissing at me!"

"C'mon, man," Mutt said. "It's just a rat snake!"

"Rat snakes aren't this big!" Indy said.

Mutt looked at Marion.

"What's with him?" he asked. "I was starting to think he wasn't afraid of anything."

"Childhood trauma," she explained. "Indy, will you just grab it!"

Indy closed his eyes, and held on to the snake and Mutt heaved him out.

"Afraid of snakes," Mutt said flatly. "You are one crazy old geezer."

Marion went pale. Two Russian soldiers were standing over her. Behind them, Oxley was standing between Spalko and Mac.

"I brought help," said Oxley.

The trucks, jeeps and amphibious vehicles had been travelling for more than a day, following the river. Spalko was riding in a truck with Mac and Oxley. The skull, inside a sack, was beside her. Suddenly everyone in the convoy heard Mutt scream in anger and confusion.

"You've got to be kidding me!" he yelled.

He, Indy and Marion were sitting tied up in the back of a covered truck. Dovchenko was sitting with them.

"My father was a British RAF pilot," Mutt insisted. "He was a *war hero*! Not some... *school*teacher!"

"I'm sorry, sweetheart," Marion said. "Colin was your stepfather. We started dating when you were three months old. He was a good man, but he wasn't your father."

"Wait a minute," Indy butted in. "Colin *Williams*? You married *him*? I introduced you two!"

Dovchenko rolled his eyes.

"You gave up your vote on who I married when you decided to break it off a week before our wedding," Marion snapped.

"It just wasn't going to work, Marion," said Indy. "Who would want to be married to somebody who's gone half the time?"

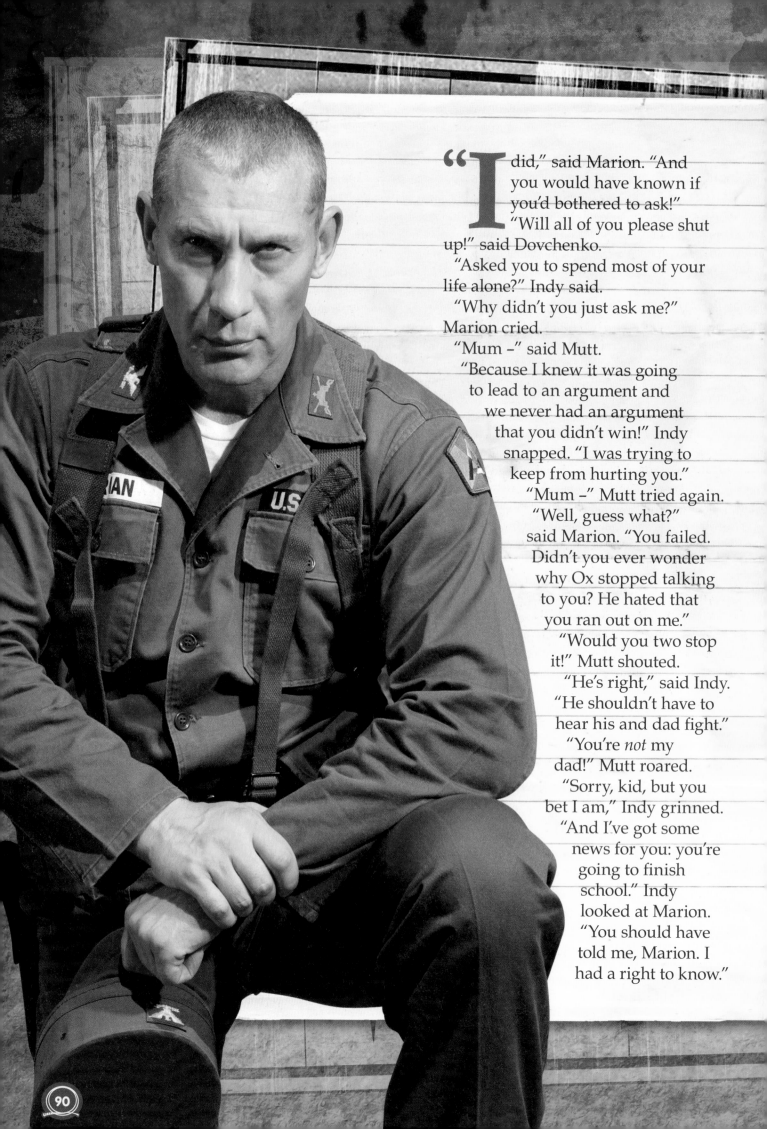

"I did," said Marion. "And you would have known if you'd bothered to ask!"

"Will all of you please shut up!" said Dovchenko.

"Asked you to spend most of your life alone?" Indy said.

"Why didn't you just ask me?" Marion cried.

"Mum –" said Mutt.

"Because I knew it was going to lead to an argument and we never had an argument that you didn't win!" Indy snapped. "I was trying to keep from hurting you."

"Mum –" Mutt tried again.

"Well, guess what?" said Marion. "You failed. Didn't you ever wonder why Ox stopped talking to you? He hated that you ran out on me."

"Would you two stop it!" Mutt shouted.

"He's right," said Indy. "He shouldn't have to hear his and dad fight."

"You're *not* my dad!" Mutt roared.

"Sorry, kid, but you bet I am," Indy grinned. "And I've got some news for you: you're going to finish school." Indy looked at Marion. "You should have told me, Marion. I had a right to know."

Dovchenko had heard enough. He put his gun down and pulled some rags out of one of the crates. He made a gag and squatted down next to Marion. Indy seized the moment and kicked the Russian in the face. Dovchenko fell towards Mutt, who kicked him back towards Indy. With another well-aimed kick, Indy knocked the Russian out. Indy used Mutt's knife to free himself and then turned to Marion and cut her loose.

"I wasn't the only one who moved on," she said. "I'm sure there were plenty of women for you over the years."

"A few," he admitted. "But all of them had the same problem. They weren't you, honey."

Indy threw the driver out of the truck and sped after the rest of the Russian vehicles.

"We have to get Oxley," he said. "Get our hands on that skull and get to Akator before Spalko does."

"Just like that, huh?" Mutt said.

"Marion, take the wheel," Indy said.

Before she could argue he had disappeared into the back of the truck.

"What's he going to do next?" asked Mutt.

"I don't think he plans that far ahead," said his mother with a grin.

Indy clambered back into the front of the truck holding a bazooka. He blew up the lead vehicle and half the vehicles in the convoy crashed into one another.

"Pull up alongside the duck!" Indy yelled, pointing at an amphibious vehicle ahead of them.

Marion did as he asked and Indy leaped on to the front of the duck.

Indy threw the soldiers from the duck and then Marion and Mutt leapt aboard. As Spalko leaped into a smaller jeep and fired on the duck, Indy sped past her and reached the truck containing Mac and Oxley. Marion took the wheel and Indy launched himself into the truck, breaking Mac's nose again. Indy sent the truck up and over a toppled tree, throwing the soldiers off. The sack containing the crystal skull flew from the rear seat, but Oxley caught it and pulled it tightly to his chest.

"You idiot!" Mac roared, clutching his nose. "I'm CIA! I practically shouted it to you in the tent! I said, 'Like in Berlin'. And what were we in Berlin? *Double agents!*"

Behind them, a soldier had managed to haul himself into the jeep. He snatched the sack from Oxley and hurled it towards Spalko. Mac threw him from the truck.

Spalko drew her sword, but before she could think about chasing Indy, something flashed next to her. Mutt Williams was alongside her vehicle with a sword in his hand! Standing in the front seat of the duck, Mutt swung at her again, and they began to duel.

Mutt leaped into Spalko's jeep and threw her into the back of the duck. He grabbed the sack containing the skull while Marion slammed her foot down on the brake pedal, catapulting Spalko and her deadly blade clear out of the duck and on to the deck. Marion rammed the duck into the back of the jeep, sending Spalko sailing back into the jeep with Mutt.

Their fierce duel continued and the sack changed hands several times, but eventually Spalko grabbed the sack and pushed Mutt on to the bonnet of Indy's truck. Then a low-hanging branch hit the boy and spun him up into the trees!

Mutt swung through the trees to catch up with the vehicles, which raced along the edge of a sheer cliff, several hundred feet above the river. Spalko took the wheel and tried to force Indy's truck off the cliff. Mutt swung into the front seat beside Spalko, grabbed the sack and leaped into the back of Indy's truck.

The two vehicles raced towards an enormous mound of dirt. Indy braked, but not soon enough. His truck bounded over a rotting log, flew into the air and came down hard on the side of the mound, stalling. Spalko's jeep sailed over them and crashed much closer to the top of the mound. As Spalko drew a pistol, a huge ant sank its pincers into her hand. Then thousands more ants began to surge into the jeep. The mound was a giant ants' nest!

"Army ants!" Indy yelled in a panic. "Everyone out!"

They all raced away from the mound as Dovchenko drove up and hurled himself at Indy. Marion screeched up in the duck and pulled Mac and Mutt aboard, then drove down towards the river and came to a low cliff, where she stopped. Halfway down the cliff, a large, leafy tree jutted out above the raging river. Marion turned the duck around and drove back towards the ants.

Dovchenko was choking Indy when Oxley pulled the crystal skull from the sack. The river of ants divided into two streams around the skull, leaving Indy, Dovchenko and Oxley untouched. Indy managed to throw Dovchenko into the middle of the mass of ants. They carried Dovchenko into their nest, and he would never be seen again. Just in time, Marion picked Indy and Oxley up and then sped towards the river.

Spalko and her other soldiers were rappelling over the edge of the cliff.

"Er, honey," Indy said, "you've got to stop this thing or we're going over the edge."

"That's the idea," she told him.

"Bad idea!" said Indy. "Give me the wheel."

"Trust me," Marion said.

"Three times it drops," Oxley said in excitement. "Drop! Drop! Drop!"

They plunged over the edge...

and then landed in the branches of the huge tree that was growing out of the side of the cliff. The duck started to rock forwards and backwards. Eventually the duck dropped free and the tree sprang back, swatting a few of the rappelling soldiers.

The duck plunged into the water and sped into the centre of the river, drawn by the current.

"Way to go, Mum!" Mutt said.

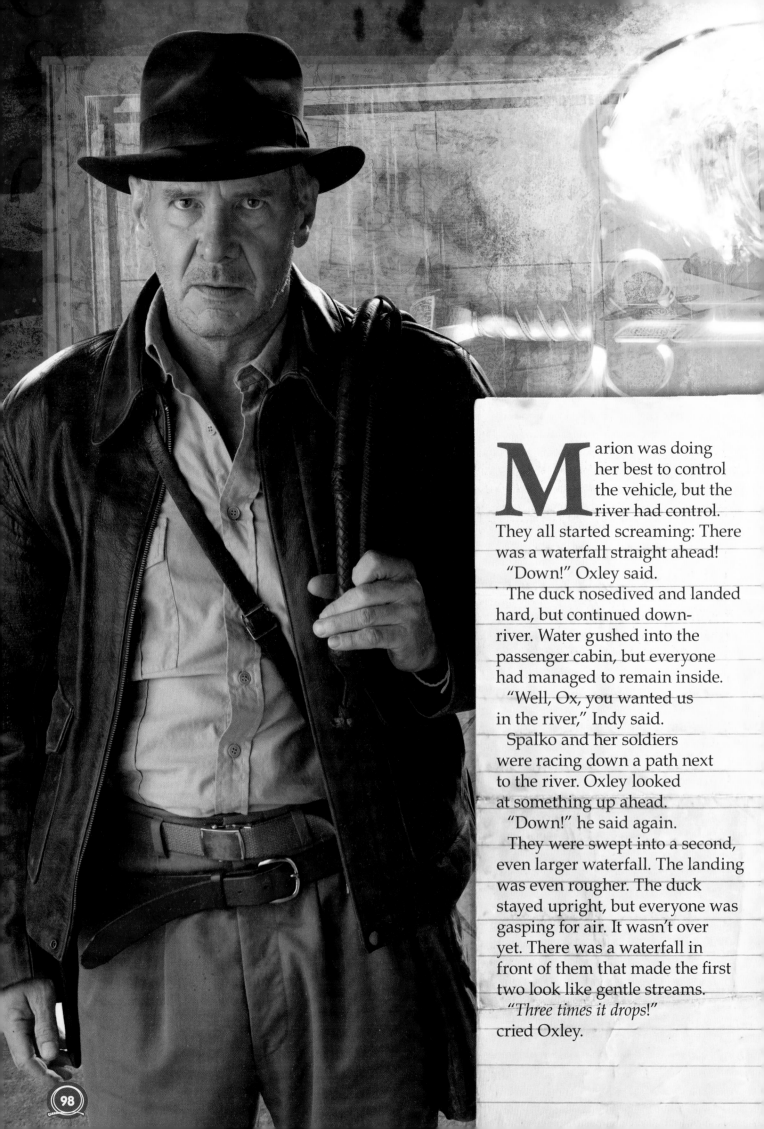

Marion was doing her best to control the vehicle, but the river had control. They all started screaming: There was a waterfall straight ahead!

"Down!" Oxley said.

The duck nosedived and landed hard, but continued downriver. Water gushed into the passenger cabin, but everyone had managed to remain inside.

"Well, Ox, you wanted us in the river," Indy said.

Spalko and her soldiers were racing down a path next to the river. Oxley looked at something up ahead.

"Down!" he said again.

They were swept into a second, even larger waterfall. The landing was even rougher. The duck stayed upright, but everyone was gasping for air. It wasn't over yet. There was a waterfall in front of them that made the first two look like gentle streams.

"*Three times it drops!*" cried Oxley.

There was no way to keep the vehicle upright. They were all thrown into the water!

After tumbling through the waves, Indy and the others dragged themselves up on to a sandy bank. The river had brought them to a wooded area surrounded by cliffs. Oxley stared at the cliff behind them. It looked like a giant head, with a waterfall flowing from one of its eye sockets.

"Through eyes that last I saw in tears," Oxley said.

"Now I remember!" Mutt said suddenly. "It's from a poem by T.S. Eliot. Through eyes in *tears*! That's the entrance to Akator – through the waterfall!"

"We're going up there," said Indy. "The skull has to be returned."

"Returned?" Marion said.

"You don't have to come," Indy said, getting to his feet.

"Why does it have to be returned?" asked Mutt.

"Why you?" Marion added.

Indy stared at them. "Because it asked me to."

Oxley climbed up the cliff, heading for the waterfall that spilled from the left eye. Indy and the others followed as fast as they could. Ahead, through the mist, they saw Oxley plunge through the water and vanish into the rock.

The others followed Oxley and found themselves in a tunnel. Its walls were covered in paintings, telling the story of what had happened long ago. The first panel showed a group of human figures – the Ugha warriors – gazing at a tall, glowing, humanoid figure that was descending from the sky. The next showed twelve more humanoid figures intermingling with the humans, building, farming, healing the sick. Their long heads matched the shape of the crystal skull.

The next painting showed the Ugha battling with invaders.

"The conquistadors," Mutt said. "Searching for El Dorado."

In the final panel, one of the thirteen humanoid figures was headless and the invaders were carrying off his skull. The thirteen humanoids were dying.

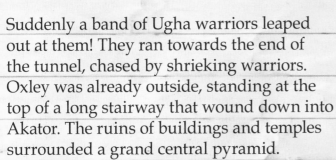

Suddenly a band of Ugha warriors leaped out at them! They ran towards the end of the tunnel, chased by shrieking warriors. Oxley was already outside, standing at the top of a long stairway that wound down into Akator. The ruins of buildings and temples surrounded a grand central pyramid.

Two warriors slammed Indy to the ground and Mutt threw them off. Another warrior leaped on Marion's back and tore at her hair. Indy used his whip to yank the warrior off and sent him sprawling into a stone wall. Elsewhere, Mac was battling three warriors. More warriors appeared every minute.

"How did you get past them?" Indy shouted to Oxley. "What do we do?"

Oxley opened the sack, took out the skull and held it up. The warriors stopped their attack, staring at the skull in wonder and fear.

Indy and his friends ran towards the central pyramid and began to climb up. It was a steep climb but at last they reached the flat top, where they found a large, square basin filled with sand. There were four enormous obelisks lying in the sand with their bases touching. Indy guessed that a single obelisk had been broken into four parts, the ends supported on stone pillars.

"It's a puzzle," said Indy. We have to reassemble the original obelisk."

Indy noticed wooden plugs set into each of the four walls. He knocked one of the wooden plugs out, and a thick stream of sand flowed from the basin. Then a grating sound filled the air and the ends of the obelisks began to rise. Eagerly, Indy, Mac and Mutt removed all the plugs. Sand spilled out over the flat roof and the obelisks continued to rise.

Finally, the four pieces came together and made a single column. The floor of the basin opened, and they saw a chamber dropping down into the pyramid. The obelisk was just the tip of a column that rose one hundred feet from the floor of the pyramid.

There was a narrow walkway spiralling down walls of the column. They began to walk down it, faster and faster, as the walkway retracted into the column. They dropped the last few feet and found themselves in the heart of the pyramid.

There were several corridors leading off from the chamber and Indy decided to explore one of them. As they descended, greenish lights illuminating their way, the carvings and adornments on the walls became more and more incredible. In one room they found plaques of pure silver, inset with garnets, opals, jade and other precious stones.

"Now this is more like it," Mac said.

He began to stuff his pockets with treasures.

Indy walked on until he saw two enormous doors. Above the doors, seven feet from the floor, was an empty recess. Indy guessed that the skull would open the door. He fitted it into the recess and the skull began to glow. Then the door groaned open to reveal the pyramid's throne room.

Indy pulled the skull from the recess and gave it back to Oxley. Then he entered the throne room. It was circular and made of stone. Thirteen tall figures stood on a raised altar.

"Let me guess. The skull's his," Mutt said.

Oxley began to walk towards the headless figure. Indy stepped to one side and then heard a click. Mac had drawn his pistol.

"Sorry, Indy," he said.

Irina Spalko walked into the throne room with three Russian soldiers. Mac had been leaving tracking devices for them to follow. He was working for the Russians after all!

Spalko took the crystal skull from Oxley.

"Imagine what they'll be able to tell us," she said.

"I can't," Indy said. "Neither could the people who were instructed to build this temple and neither can you."

"*Belief*, Dr Jones," she said, moving towards the figure without a head. "It is a gift you have yet to receive."

"Oh, I believe, sister," Indy said. "That's why I'm staying down here."

As Spalko reached the altar stairs, something tore the skull out of her grasp. It returned to the neck of the figure that had been without it for so long. There was a deep boom and the circular wall began to shake. Carvings smashed on the stone floor. Bricks crumbled and the stone wall fell down. Behind it was another, very different, surface. It looked metallic, but it was like nothing Indy had ever seen before. The thirteen beings were shaking. They were coming to life!

Tell me everything you know!" Spalko demanded. "I want it all!"

The thirteen turned to look at her, and their eyes were glowing fiercely.

"I've got a bad feeling about this," Indy said, taking a step back.

"What is it?" Mutt asked. "What are they, spacemen?"

"Inter-dimensional beings, in point of fact," Oxley said.

Indy smiled, realising that his friend had returned to normal.

"Welcome back, Ox," he said.

The strange walls of the throne room started to spin. A whirlpool manifested in the centre of the room, sucking debris and metal into it, incredibly magnetic.

"What the hell is that thing?" Marion screamed.

"A portal," said Oxley. "A pathway."

"A problem!" Indy said.

Indy ran out of the throne room, Mutt, Marion and Oxley right behind him. Spalko drew closer to the edge of the whirlpool portal. Her soldiers were sucked in and destroyed, but she didn't care. Mac dashed from the throne room after Indy.

Spalko could not escape. Some strange force had entered her and was consuming her.

"I can see! I can see it all!" She screamed as infinite knowledge poured into her, more powerful than the fires of the sun, and more destructive.

"I can see everything!" she shrieked.

Smoke came from her boiling eyes as she breathed for the last time. At the same moment, the portal began to swell, and the thirteen crystal beings vanished into another dimension.

Indy and the others raced towards the central chamber. The corridor was shaking so much that they could hardly stay on their feet, and the passageways were filling with water. Just as Mutt, Marion and Oxley entered the central chamber, Mac slipped and fell. Indy skidded and turned around. Mac was a traitor, but Indy couldn't leave him behind.

Mac was being pulled back. All the jewels he had stolen were being magnetically sucked back by the powerful tug of the portal. Indy tried desperately to save his old friend, but he wasn't strong enough. Mac was sucked into the portal!

The walls of the central chamber cracked and water began to pour in from all sides, lifting Indy and his friends upwards. At last they were thrown out of the pyramid, landing on a grassy slope near the cliff they had climbed. Akator was collapsing and everything was whirling around in the air. The four survivors watched in wonder as water began flooding the city, turning Akator into a mountain lake.

Indy groaned in pain, sat down and leaned against a tree. He held an arm out for Marion, and she crawled over to him and put her head on his shoulder.

"So we're just gonna sit here?" said Mutt.

"Night falls quickly in the jungle, kid," Indy said. "We can't climb down in the dark."

"Says who?" said Mutt, standing up.

Indy pushed his hat back and looked at the boy.

"Why don't you stick around, Junior?" he said with a lopsided grin.

"I don't know," said Mutt. "Why didn't you, *Dad*?"

Indy groaned.

"Somewhere my old man is laughing," he said.

Harold Oxley, Stanforth, many of Indy's colleagues and some of his students were in the church to see Indy and Marion marry at last. As the minister pronounced them man and wife, Indy clasped Marion in his arms and kissed her. Organ music began to play and the wooden doors of the church were thrown open.

A sudden breeze blew Indy's fedora from a hat rack and sent it tumbling down the aisle, where it stopped at the toes of a pair of motorcycle boots. Mutt picked the hat up and dusted it off. Then he raised it to his head. However, a hand reached out and took it. Throwing Mutt a grin, Indy put the hat where it belonged: on his own head.

There were plenty more adventures to be had – but this was the start of the greatest adventure of them all!

ANSWERS

PAGE 20

1.
2.
3.
4.
5.

PAGE 21

NOTE 1: DEAR INDY, THE SECRET TREASURE IS BURIED IN PERU. FROM MAC.

NOTE 2: TO INDIANA JONES, BEWARE! YOU ARE IN GREAT DANGER! A FRIEND.

NOTE 3: THE NAZIS HAVE FOUND MY HIDING PLACE. SAVE ME, INDY!

NOTE 4: DR JONES, YOU WILL NEVER SUCCEED.

NOTE 5: JUNIOR, KEEP THIS DIARY SAFE. DO NOT LET IT OUT OF YOUR SIGHT! DAD.

PAGE 22

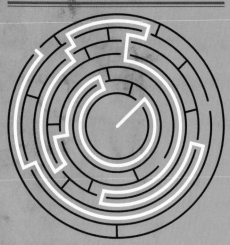

PAGE 23

ABNER
EGYPT
OXLEY
ARCHAEOLOGY
STONES
QUEST

PAGE 30

PAGE 31

TELL INDIANA JONES THAT HIS FATHER HAS BEEN KIDNAPPED.
THE ENEMY HAS TAKEN THE ARK.
THE CHILDREN HAVE BEEN HIDDEN IN THE TEMPLE.
ONLY DR JONES CAN SAVE THE GRAIL.
THE CRYSTAL SKULL IS VERY POWERFUL.

A	B	C	D	E	F	G	H	I	J	K	L	M
K	F	X	P	N	J	H	C	R	S	I	Q	W

N	O	P	Q	R	S	T	U	V	W	X	Y	Z
T	Z	B	O	A	Y	V	M	D	U	G	E	L

PAGE 32

B & F

PAGE 33

A	N	G	C	O	A	D	V	E	N	T	U	R	E	F	L	I	G	N	C
E	I	P	A	U	D	Y	N	K	F	Y	B	L	A	U	D	L	V	I	H
H	S	N	V	D	D	N	V	A	K	C	S	J	C	E	P	F	H	O	J
L	J	P	D	J	T	A	E	H	S	A	K	A	T	O	R	C	N	I	F
D	R	F	S	Z	Q	G	R	J	U	K	J	D	A	R	Y	C	A	Q	L
Q	I	T	D	T	A	O	A	Q	D	S	I	H	S	G	L	U	D	H
B	V	B	N	U	J	M	H	M	F	K	E	I	P	S	B	F	C	A	G
K	U	I	V	B	Y	G	A	E	J	A	J	P	U	D	F	S	M	R	F
E	A	O	R	P	D	R	I	V	A	I	E	Q	H	Q	T	U	K	J	Q
L	Y	F	O	J	I	G	E	E	R	U	S	A	E	R	T	E	Y	C	J
C	O	L	K	O	B	T	F	N	T	E	Y	L	C	T	J	A	K	U	O
N	A	Q	N	J	J	P	A	T	E	G	B	F	Y	F	V	J	N	I	H
R	F	K	E	U	E	D	C	G	F	V	Y	N	H	L	C	I	F	A	N
I	U	Q	H	D	S	J	H	I	A	J	K	E	B	R	O	J	O	G	B
B	K	L	C	Q	F	P	L	E	C	D	H	R	R	N	D	B	V	K
H	J	F	V	H	J	U	A	Q	T	I	E	A	Y	X	Q	K	P	U	G
N	O	P	O	R	A	G	O	L	S	J	F	N	J	O	O	E	S	R	K
G	L	D	D	L	C	U	F	T	K	O	E	B	T	F	S	N	G	E	D
A	K	C	Q	I	J	I	P	B	S	O	T	B	D	V	A	J	Y	P	Q
G	S	N	A	K	E	S	H	F	N	D	K	E	J	G	K	T	D	P	I

PAGE 74